GOSCINNY AND UDERZO

PRESENT

An Asterix Adventure

ASTERIX AND THE ROMAN AGENT

Written by RENÉ GOSCINNY *and Illustrated by* ALBERT UDERZO

Translated by Anthea Bell *and* Derek Hockridge

Asterix titles available now

1 Asterix the Gaul
2 Asterix and the Golden Sickle
3 Asterix and the Goths
4 Asterix the Gladiator
5 Asterix and the Banquet
6 Asterix and Cleopatra
7 Asterix and the Big Fight
8 Asterix in Britain
9 Asterix and the Normans
10 Asterix the Legionary
11 Asterix and the Chieftain's Shield
12 Asterix at the Olympic Games
13 Asterix and the Cauldron
14 Asterix in Spain
15 Asterix and the Roman Agent
16 Asterix in Switzerland
17 The Mansions of the Gods
18 Asterix and the Laurel Wreath
19 Asterix and the Soothsayer
20 Asterix in Corsica
21 Asterix and Caesar's Gift
22 Asterix and the Great Crossing
23 Obelix and Co.
24 Asterix in Belgium
25 Asterix and the Great Divide
26 Asterix and the Black Gold
27 Asterix and Son
28 Asterix and the Magic Carpet
29 Asterix and the Secret Weapon
30 Asterix and Obelix All at Sea
31 Asterix and the Actress
32 Asterix and the Class Act
33 Asterix and the Falling Sky
34 Asterix and Obelix's Birthday – the Golden Book
35 Asterix and the Picts

Where's Asterix?
Where's Dogmatix?
Asterix and the Vikings
Asterix at the Olympic Games (film tie-in)
Asterix Omnibus 1 (Books 1-3)
Asterix Omnibus 2 (Books 4-6)
Asterix Omnibus 3 (Books 7-9)
Asterix Omnibus 4 (Books 10-12)
Asterix Omnibus 5 (Books 13-15)
Asterix Omnibus 6 (Books 16-18)
Asterix Omnibus 7 (Books 19-21)
Asterix Omnibus 8 (Books 22-24)
Asterix Omnibus 9 (Books 25-27)
Asterix Omnibus 10 (Books 28-30)
Asterix Omnibus 11 (Books 31-33)
How Obelix Fell into the Magic Potion

Original title: *La Zizanie*

Exclusive licensee: Orion Publishing Group
Translators: Anthea Bell and Derek Hockridge
Typography: Bryony Newhouse

This revised edition first published in 2004 by Orion Books Ltd,
Orion House, 5 Upper Saint Martin's Lane, London WC2H 9EA
An Hachette UK company

13 15 17 19 20 18 16 14 12

Printed in China

www.asterix.com
www.orionbooks.co.uk

A CIP record for this book is available from the British Library

ISBN 978-0-7528-6632-1 (cased)
ISBN 978-0-7528-6633-8 (paperback)
ISBN 978-1-4440-1311-1 (ebook)

The Orion Publishing Group's policy is to use papers that are natural, renewable and recyclable products and made from wood grown in sustainable forests. The logging and manufacturing processes are expected to conform to the environmental regulations of the country of origin.

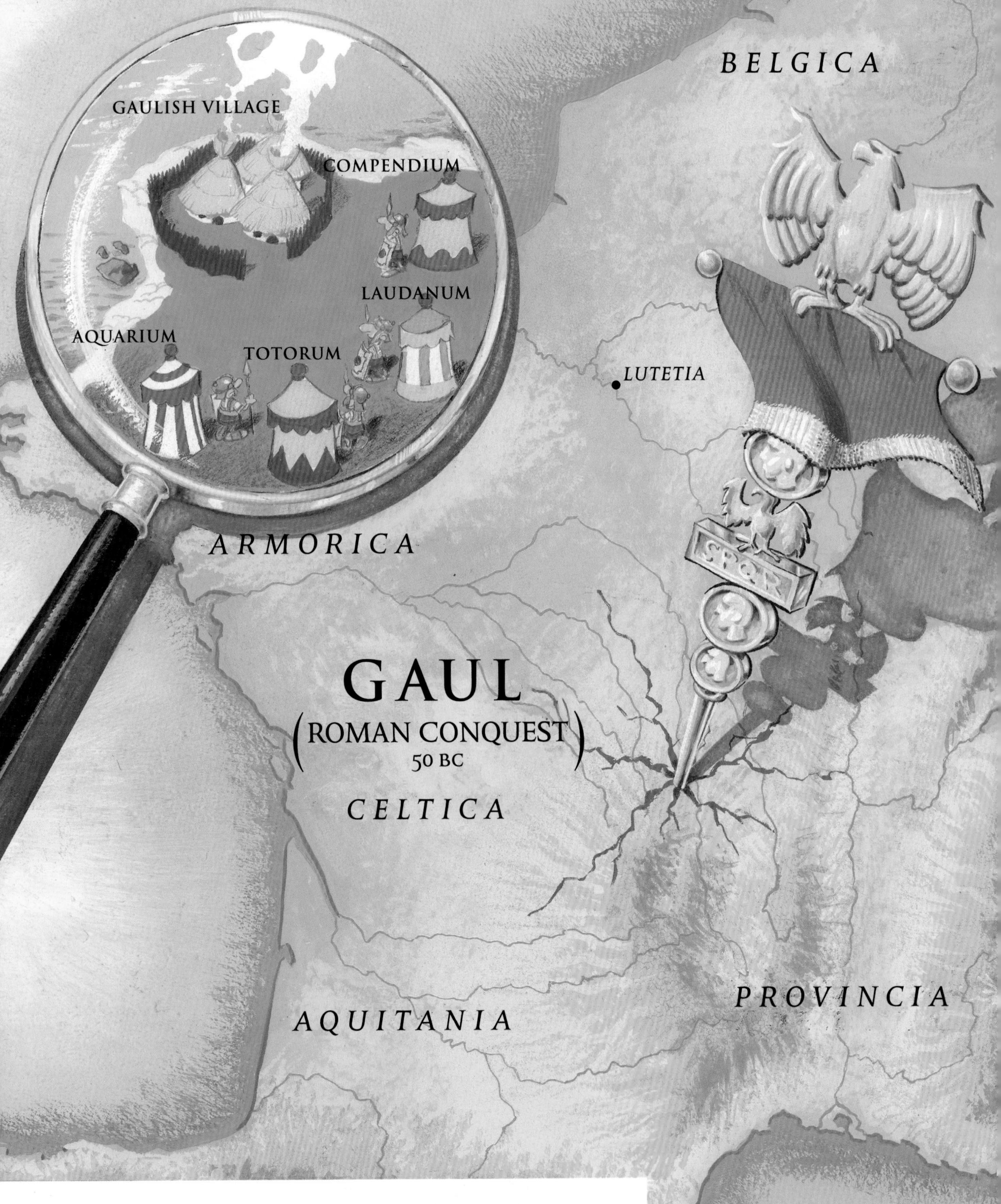

THE YEAR IS 50 BC. GAUL IS ENTIRELY OCCUPIED BY THE ROMANS. WELL, NOT ENTIRELY ... ONE SMALL VILLAGE OF INDOMITABLE GAULS STILL HOLDS OUT AGAINST THE INVADERS. AND LIFE IS NOT EASY FOR THE ROMAN LEGIONARIES WHO GARRISON THE FORTIFIED CAMPS OF TOTORUM, AQUARIUM, LAUDANUM AND COMPENDIUM ...

ASTERIX, THE HERO OF THESE ADVENTURES. A SHREWD, CUNNING LITTLE WARRIOR, ALL PERILOUS MISSIONS ARE IMMEDIATELY ENTRUSTED TO HIM. ASTERIX GETS HIS SUPERHUMAN STRENGTH FROM THE MAGIC POTION BREWED BY THE DRUID GETAFIX . . .

OBELIX, ASTERIX'S INSEPARABLE FRIEND. A MENHIR DELIVERY MAN BY TRADE, ADDICTED TO WILD BOAR. OBELIX IS ALWAYS READY TO DROP EVERYTHING AND GO OFF ON A NEW ADVENTURE WITH ASTERIX – SO LONG AS THERE'S WILD BOAR TO EAT, AND PLENTY OF FIGHTING. HIS CONSTANT COMPANION IS DOGMATIX, THE ONLY KNOWN CANINE ECOLOGIST, WHO HOWLS WITH DESPAIR WHEN A TREE IS CUT DOWN.

GETAFIX, THE VENERABLE VILLAGE DRUID, GATHERS MISTLETOE AND BREWS MAGIC POTIONS. HIS SPECIALITY IS THE POTION WHICH GIVES THE DRINKER SUPERHUMAN STRENGTH. BUT GETAFIX ALSO HAS OTHER RECIPES UP HIS SLEEVE . . .

CACOFONIX, THE BARD. OPINION IS DIVIDED AS TO HIS MUSICAL GIFTS. CACOFONIX THINKS HE'S A GENIUS. EVERYONE ELSE THINKS HE'S UNSPEAKABLE. BUT SO LONG AS HE DOESN'T SPEAK, LET ALONE SING, EVERYBODY LIKES HIM . . .

FINALLY, VITALSTATISTIX, THE CHIEF OF THE TRIBE. MAJESTIC, BRAVE AND HOT-TEMPERED, THE OLD WARRIOR IS RESPECTED BY HIS MEN AND FEARED BY HIS ENEMIES. VITALSTATISTIX HIMSELF HAS ONLY ONE FEAR, HE IS AFRAID THE SKY MAY FALL ON HIS HEAD TOMORROW. BUT AS HE ALWAYS SAYS, TOMORROW NEVER COMES.

ALL IS PEACEFUL IN THE LITTLE GAULISH VILLAGE WE KNOW SO WELL, AND, AS USUAL, EVERYONE IS CHEERFUL AND FRIENDLY...
GOOD MORNING, OBELIX, GOOD MORNING, DOGMATIX!
GOOD MORNING, ASTERIX!
WOOF!
GOOD MORNING, UNHYGIENIX!
GOOD MORNING, IMPEDIMENTA!
UNHYGIENIX FISHMONGER
GOOD MORNING, GERIATRIX!
GOOD MORNING, CACOFONIX! STILL LOST YOUR VOICE?
GOOD MORNING, MY BOY!
AND IN THE ROMAN SENATE, OLD SENATOR STRADIVARIUS IS GETTING ALL STRUNG UP. IN HIS WELL MODULATED TONES, CALCULATED TO ROUSE A CROWD TO FEVER PITCH, HE IS SETTLING AN OLD SCORE WITH CAESAR...
CAESAR STILL ASKS US FOR MONEY AND MEN TO WAGE WAR, AND YET HE'S NOT EVEN CAPABLE OF KEEPING THE PAX ROMANA IN THE COUNTRIES HE'S ALREADY CONQUERED! ...
...THERE'S A LITTLE VILLAGE UP THERE IN GAUL. IT DEFIES OUR OCCUPYING FORCES AND REFUSES TO OBEY OUR LAWS!
LET CAESAR ENFORCE THE POWER OF ROME IN THE OCCUPIED TERRITORIES BEFORE HE THINKS OF NEW CAMPAIGNS!
YES!
HEAR, HEAR!
FOR JUPITER'S SAKE, GET THAT PLEB A SEAT!
A PLEBISCITE! GOOD IDEA!
SO THE NEXT DAY CAESAR HOLDS A MEETING OF HIS FRIENDS AND COLLEAGUES AT HIS LUXURIOUS VILLA OUTSIDE ROME.
MON REPOS
MEA REQVIES
CAVE CANEM
BEWARE OF THE DOG

AH, THERE YOU ARE AT LAST, BRUTUS! SIT DOWN. NOW WE CAN BEGIN.
THE ROADS ARE SO BUSY AFTER THE CALENDS...
THE SENATE WANTS TO TAKE ITS REVENGE ON ME FOR CUTTING ITS POWER. I MUST SHOW THEM WHO'S THE BOSS, AND TO DO THAT I'LL HAVE TO WIPE OUT THIS WRETCHED GAULISH VILLAGE...
LET'S HAVE YOUR IDEAS... SPEAK UP.
ET TU, BRUTE.
I SUGGEST BRUTE FORCE!
THEY HAVE A MAGIC POTION WHICH MAKES THEM INVINCIBLE. AND DO PUT THAT DAGGER AWAY, YOU IDIOT, YOU'LL DO YOURSELF AN INJURY!
STOP ME IF I'M ON THE WRONG TRACK, BUT WHAT ABOUT BUYING THEM OFF?
THESE BARBARIANS ARE NOT INTERESTED IN MONEY. IF THEY WERE, THE MAGIC POTION WOULD HAVE BEEN ON THE MARKET LONG AGO!
THIS IS ONLY A SUGGESTION, BUT...
...THEIR STRENGTH SPRINGS FROM THEIR SOLIDARITY. IF WE COULD SOW A BIT OF DISCORD IN THE VILLAGE, THEY WOULD SPLIT UP AND THE POTION WOULDN'T MATTER ANY MORE...
I KNOW THE GAULS ARE FAMOUS FOR THEIR INCESSANT ARGUMENTS, BUT THIS LOT STICK TOGETHER THROUGH THICK AND THIN.
J.C.! I'VE GOT THE VERY MAN! HE'LL SPLIT THEM UP FOR YOU!
HE USED TO HAVE A FLAT IN AN INSULA* I OWN. HE MADE SO MUCH TROUBLE IN THE BUILDING THAT THE OTHER TENANTS MANAGED TO GET HIM THROWN INTO PRISON TO BE EATEN BY THE LIONS!
* BLOCK OF FLATS
WHERE IS THIS TROUBLEMAKER OF YOURS?
HE'S STILL IN PRISON. WHEN THEY PUT HIM IN THE ARENA, THE LIONS ATE ONE ANOTHER!
HAVE HIM BROUGHT TO ME! NOW FOR SOME FOOD. ET TU, BRUTE!
THESE CLASSICAL ALLUSIONS ARE BEGINNING TO GET ON MY NERVES! ONE OF THESE DAYS I'LL...

WHAT'S HIS NAME, YOUR TROUBLEMAKER?
TORTUOUS CONVOLVULUS. YOU'LL SEE, J.C. HE'S A BIT OF A WEED, BUT VERY EFFECTIVE. THE GREEN-EYED MONSTER FOLLOWS HIM WHEREVER HE GOES – IT'S LIKE MAGIC!
WE NEED MAGIC TO GET RID OF THOSE GAULS...
YOU'RE A ROTTEN SNEAK, BY JUPITER!
SAY THAT AGAIN!
WHAT'S HAPPENING OUT THERE?!?
YOU HEARD – A ROTTEN SNEAK!
I'LL TEACH YOU TO GO ROUND SAYING I'M THE CENTURION'S PET!
IS THAT SO? AND WHO WAS IT TOLD HIM I CAME BACK TO CAMP I OVER THE VIII LAST NIGHT?
?
NOW THEN, WHAT'S ALL THIS ABOUT?
IT WASN'T ME WHO ...
AVE CAESAR! IN ACCORDANCE WITH OUR ORDERS WE HAVE BROUGHT YOU THE PRISONER TORTUOUS CONVOLVULUS.
CLAC!
GOOD. UNDO HIM, THEN FALL OUT.
COME ALONG, TORTUOUS CONVOLVULUS.
SNEAK!
DRUNKARD!

YOU MEAN THIS IS THE ANSWER TO ALL OUR PROBLEMS? HE DOESN'T LOOK UP TO MUCH!
OH, YES, THAT'S RIGHT! WHEN IT'S NOT BRUTUS'S IDEA, BRUTUS IS JEALOUS!
JEALOUS? MAYBE I AM JEALOUS, BUT I DIDN'T BETRAY CAESAR! I WAS NEVER IN THE PAY OF POMPEY!
ME IN POMPEY'S PAY? HE MAY HAVE BEEN, NOT TO MENTION ANY NAMES, AND HIM, AND HIM! BUT I NEVER BETRAYED J.C.!
IF YOU DON'T MIND! HE WAS A TRAITOR, NOT ME!
ARE YOU OFF YOUR HEAD?
TAP! TAP! TAP!
LIAR!!!
FANCY SUSPECTING ME! ME, WHEN I DENOUNCED EVERYONE ELSE!
HOW INTERESTING!
HEE, HEE, HEE!
TRAITOR!
BARBARIAN!
DIRTY SPY!
GENTLEMEN, PLEASE! I SHOULDN'T LIKE TO BE THE CAUSE OF ANY DISAGREEMENT. IF, IN THE PAST, YOU HAVE TAKEN ADVANTAGE OF CAESAR'S GULLIBILITY...
GULLIBLE, ME???
YOU'RE GREAT! I'M SENDING YOU ON A MISSION TO GAUL. IF YOU SUCCEED YOU'LL GET YOUR FREEDOM AND A FORTUNE.
CROOK!
PROFITEER!
SCOUNDREL!
TRAITOR!

MEANWHILE, THINGS ARE MUCH THE SAME IN THE LITTLE GAULISH VILLAGE...
LIFE'S GOOD, O DRUID!
TOO GOOD, ASTERIX! THE ROMANS ARE BEHAVING THEMSELVES, WE HAVEN'T GOT ANY WORRIES, OUR BARD HAS LOST HIS VOICE – IT CAN'T LAST... I FEEL THERE'S TROUBLE BREWING.
OUR DRUID'S CHANGED! HE'S GETTING PESSIMISTIC IN HIS OLD AGE.
HOWEVER, THE DRUID'S PREMONITION IS NOT WITHOUT FOUNDATION. DANGER IS PLOUGHING ITS WAY TOWARDS GAUL ON BOARD A ROMAN GALLEY WHERE EVERYONE IS ARGUING, FROM THE CAPTAIN...
WELL NOW, ABERDEENANGUS, SO IT SEEMS I'M NOTHING BUT AN OLD AMPHORA OF WINE?
I NEVER SAID THAT, CAP'N! IT WAS GIANTORTUS WHO SAID THAT!
...DOWN TO THE GALLEY SLAVES.
WAS IT YOU WHO TOLD THE OTHER LADS I WASN'T PULLING MY WEIGHT?
SHUT UP AND ROW!
5A
WELL, GIANTORTUS DID SAY THAT IT WAS YOU WHO SAID I WAS NOTHING BUT AN OLD AMPHORA OF WINE!
AND I SAY THAT IF GIANTORTUS SAID THAT, GIANTORTUS IS A LIAR!
PIRATE SHIP TO PORT!
DID YOU HEAR THAT, CAPTAIN?
NO! NO ONE'S TO LISTEN TO HIM! HE'S BEEN SENT TO COVENTRIUM!
HE DARED TO SAY THAT WHILE WE WERE AT SEA OUR WIVES WERE ALL OUT AT ORGIES!
?!?
IF THAT'S THE WAY THE LAND LIES, I SHAN'T SAY ANOTHER WORD!!!
HUH! THEY'RE THE SORT OF PEOPLE WHO'D SAY I ONLY GOT INTO THE NAVY BECAUSE MY WIFE IS A CLOSE FRIEND OF JULIUS CAESAR'S SECOND COUSIN TWICE REMOVED!
5B

ROMAN GALLEY TO STARBOARD!
D'YOU SEE ANY GAULS?
NOT A SIGN!
RIGHT... GET READY TO BOARD HER!
THE PIRATES ARE GOING TO BOARD US, CAPTAIN! WHAT CAN WE DO?
ARE YOU EXPECTING A DECISION FROM AN OLD AMPHORA OF WINE, GIANTORTUS?
THAT'S SLANDER! ABERDEENANGUS SPENDS HIS TIME SLANDERING EVERYONE!
I'VE JUST ABOUT HAD ENOUGH...
HAVE YOU LOT DOWN THERE NEARLY FINISHED? WOULDN'T YOUR WIVES BE PROUD IF THEY COULD SEE YOU NOW!
6A
THAT'S DONE IT! COME DOWN HERE, AND JUMP TO IT!
NO! I PREFER TO REMAIN ALOOF, ALOFT!
CUT THAT MAST DOWN!!!
HEY! WHAT ABOUT US, THEN?
6B

WHAT CAN WE DO FOR YOU?
SHIVER ME TIMBERS! YOU CAN GET READY TO RECEIVE BOARDERS, THAT'S WHAT YOU CAN DO!
BUT THAT'S NOT ON! WHEN I SAW HIM IN ROME, I GAVE HIM A BAG OF GOLD AND HE PROMISED NOT TO ATTACK US!
?! ! ?!
A TRAITOR IN OUR MIDST!
TRAITOR, ME?
AND WHERE'S THE GOLD? WE NEVER SAW ANY OF IT!
HOW DARE YOU BLACKEN MY NAME!
AURI SACRA FAMES!
AS FOR YOU, YOU DISTINGUISHED CLASSICAL SCHOLAR, YOU'RE BEGINNING TO GET ON MY...
BOING!
HAAAAAA!
I'VE HOLED US IN THE HOLD! I'VE HOLED US IN THE HOLD!
GLUGGLUGGLUGGLUG
BOOM!
CRACK!
TCHAC! TCHONK!
BIFF!
BONG! PAFF!
WHAT THE... WE'RE SINKING!!!
NOW YOU'RE SCUPPERED!
PAFF!
WHAM
TCHONK!
THIS IS GREAT, BOYS! WE DON'T NEED THE GAULS ANY MORE. WE CAN MAKE FOOLS OF OURSELVES WITHOUT THEM.

IN THE LITTLE GAULISH VILLAGE, IN CONTRAST TO THESE VIOLENT EVENTS...
WE'RE GOING TO GET THINGS READY FOR CHIEF VITALSTATISTIX'S BIRTHDAY PARTY.
IT WILL BE AN OCCASION OF GENERAL GOODWILL!
THERE'LL BE HEAPS OF BOAR FULL OF BONES, DOGMATIX!
I'M GOING TO GIVE THE CHIEF A MENHIR. WHAT ABOUT YOU?
A SHIELD FOR HIS COLLECTION!
I'M GOING TO GIVE HIM A SWORD!
I'M GOING TO GIVE HIM A FISH. HE CAN STUFF IT!
DON'T LET ON! REMEMBER, WE WANT TO GIVE VITALSTATISTIX A NICE SURPRISE...
WHAT A WONDERFUL SURPRISE! MY DEAR FRIENDS...
...I AM AT A LOSS FOR WORDS, BUT LET ME TRY TO EXPRESS ALL THE JOY I FEEL...
YOU COULD HELP ME PLUCK THIS CHICKEN, INSTEAD OF SPOUTING SUCH RUBBISH!
IMPEDIMENTA, IN MY POSITION AS CHIEF, AS THE MOST IMPORTANT MAN IN THE VILLAGE, I DO HAVE CERTAIN OBLIGATIONS...
YES, WHEN IT COMES TO STUFFING YOURSELF WITH FOOD AND DRINK ANY EXCUSE WILL DO, BUT WHEN IT COMES TO WORKING...
WELL, YOU'RE PROUD OF BEING THE CHIEF'S WIFE, AREN'T YOU? FIRST LADY OF THE VILLAGE! SOME OF MY GLORY RUBS OFF ON TO YOU!
YOU CAN SAY THAT AGAIN! WE'RE GOING TO BE LANDED WITH A LOT OF STUPID PRESENTS. WE COULD NEVER EXPECT YOUR FRIENDS TO GIVE YOU ANYTHING WORTHWHILE, OH NO! NO ARTISTIC SENSE! JUST SAVAGES...

IN THE TENT OF THE CENTURION IN COMMAND OF THE ROMAN CAMP OF AQUARIUM...
...AND THAT POTION OF THEIRS MUST BE STRONG STUFF – THEY'RE FULL OF TEAM SPIRIT!
I KNOW ALL THAT, FELIX PLATYPUS. BUT YOU KNOW WHAT CAESAR SAID: YOU MUST TAKE YOUR ORDERS FROM ME!
I DON'T OBJECT TO THAT AT ALL, CONVOLVULUS. I JUST DON'T THINK THAT YOU'LL MANAGE TO SPLIT THEM UP..
YOU HAVE GIVEN ME THE NAME AND DESCRIPTION OF EVERY ONE OF THOSE NUT CASES. NOW, I NEED THAT!
THAT?
IT'S JUST THAT THIS VASE IS PART OF THE SPOILS FROM ONE OF MY CAMPAIGNS...
YES, YOUR JUNIOR OFFICERS TOLD ME YOU HAD SOME INDIVIDUAL IDEAS ABOUT SHARING OUT THE BOOTY.
GET ALL MY JUNIOR OFFICERS FALLEN IN!
SOON AFTERWARDS...
WHAT D'YOU WANT, ROMAN?
I HAVE BROUGHT A PRESENT TO THE MOST IMPORTANT MAN IN THE VILLAGE!
...AND HE'S BROUGHT A VALUABLE VASE!
AH!
?
PORTERS!
CLICK
HERE HE COMES! RIGHT, BOYS! SHOW A BIT OF DIGNITY! WE DON'T WANT TO LOOK AS IF WE'RE EXPECTING HIM!

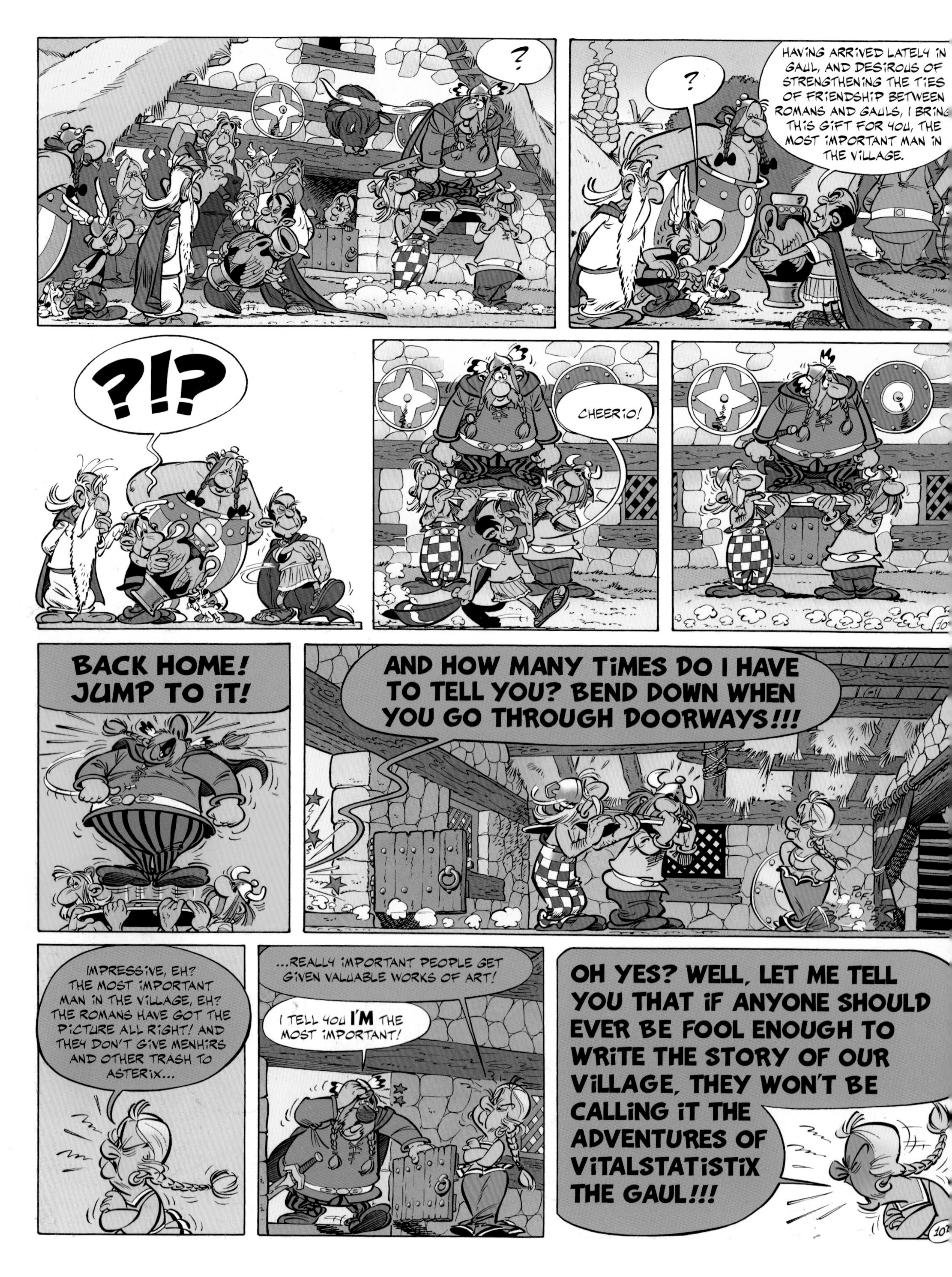
?
?
HAVING ARRIVED LATELY IN GAUL, AND DESIROUS OF STRENGTHENING THE TIES OF FRIENDSHIP BETWEEN ROMANS AND GAULS, I BRING THIS GIFT FOR YOU, THE MOST IMPORTANT MAN IN THE VILLAGE.
?!?
CHEERIO!
BACK HOME! JUMP TO IT!
AND HOW MANY TIMES DO I HAVE TO TELL YOU? BEND DOWN WHEN YOU GO THROUGH DOORWAYS!!!
IMPRESSIVE, EH? THE MOST IMPORTANT MAN IN THE VILLAGE, EH? THE ROMANS HAVE GOT THE PICTURE ALL RIGHT! AND THEY DON'T GIVE MENHIRS AND OTHER TRASH TO ASTERIX...
...REALLY IMPORTANT PEOPLE GET GIVEN VALUABLE WORKS OF ART!
I TELL YOU I'M THE MOST IMPORTANT!
OH YES? WELL, LET ME TELL YOU THAT IF ANYONE SHOULD EVER BE FOOL ENOUGH TO WRITE THE STORY OF OUR VILLAGE, THEY WON'T BE CALLING IT THE ADVENTURES OF VITALSTATISTIX THE GAUL!!!

...A VALUABLE VASE, STUDDED WITH JEWELS!
...AND FULL OF PRECIOUS STONES. I SAW THEM!
DID YOU SEE VITALSTATISTIX'S FACE?
WATCH OUT! HERE'S IMPEDIMENTA!
HYGIENIX
FISHMON
GOOD MORNING.
UNHYGIE
HEY! THERE'S A QUEUE HERE, YOU KNOW!
WHAT? BUT I'M THE CHIEF'S WIFE! THE FIRST LADY OF THE VILLAGE!
THAT'S NOT WHAT THE ROMANS THINK!
THAT'S RIGHT! IF ASTERIX WAS MARRIED, MRS ASTERIX WOULD BE IT!
BACTERIA! HELP ME GET THE FISH IN! QUICK!
OH, WOULD SHE?
YES, SHE WOULD!
LADIES! LADIES! TAKE IT EASY!
BIFF!
HIIIIIII!
SOON AFTERWARDS...

AH! WHAT HAVE YOU BROUGHT FOR LUNCH, IMPEDIMENTA, MY LOVE?
THAT!
SPLATCH!
BOOHOO! MY PARENTS WARNED ME YOU WERE NO GOOD! I'VE GIVEN THE BEST YEARS OF MY LIFE TO A GREAT FAT BOAR! A BARBARIAN! A FAILURE! EVERYONE LOOKS DOWN ON ME!
!?!?
YOU'LL NEVER GET A VALUABLE VASE, NOT YOU! NOBODY EVER GIVES ANYTHING LIKE THAT TO YOU!
I'M JUST ABOUT FED UP TO THE BACK TEETH WITH THIS VASE!
AND COARSE WITH IT! BOOHOO! BOOHOO!
WATCH IT! HERE'S THE BOSS!
?
I DIDN'T RING FOR YOU! I'M GOING OUT ON FOOT! INCOGNITO!!
!
WHAT DO YOU WANT, ROMAN?
NOTHING. I WAS JUST PASSING, SO I POPPED IN TO SAY AVE.
RIGHT. AVE. NOW TAKE YOUR VASE AND OFF YOU GO!
WOULDN'T HEAR OF IT! I WON'T KEEP YOU ANY LONGER.
THAT BOAR WAS EXCELLENT! THANKS FOR EVERYTHING ASTERIX!
?

THAT ROMAN IS CRAZY!
AH, ASTERIX! SO YOU'VE BEEN HAVING GUESTS IN TO SHARE YOUR BOAR, HAVE YOU?
HMMF!
BOING!
GUESTS? NO SUCH THING! APART FROM OBELIX, AND HE...
THAT ROMAN SEEMED TO APPRECIATE YOUR BOAR, ALL THE SAME...
HE DIDN'T TOUCH IT! COME AND SEE, O CHIEF WE HAVE TWO BOARS AND THEY HAVEN'T BEEN STARTED!
DON'T YOU EVER LET GO OF THAT VASE?
SLURP!
SCRUNCH! SCRUNCH!
WHAT THE...??!
YOU'RE FREE TO CHOOSE YOUR OWN FRIENDS, ASTERIX, EVEN IN THE ENEMY CAMP, EVEN ROMANS.
COULDN'T YOU WAIT BEFORE GOBBLING UP THOSE BOARS, YOU GREEDY PIG?
THEY WERE GETTING COLD, AND WHEN YOU WENT OUT AFTER YOUR FRIEND...
HE IS NOT MY FRIEND!
YOU'RE FREE TO CHOOSE YOUR OWN FRIENDS, ASTERIX, EVEN IN THE ENEMY CAMP, EVEN ROMANS!
I'LL BE MORE CAREFUL ABOUT CHOOSING MY FRIENDS IN FUTURE!
I GET THE MESSAGE. COME ALONG, DOGMATIX. WE'RE IN THE WAY HERE.
AVE, ASTERIX!

RIGHT, THAT'S IT. HE'S GONE TOO FAR THIS TIME. GRMMPHGROGNGROGN...
GROUMFSROGNR GROGNGROGNON...
GROGNGROGNGROGNSNNN
?
ASTERIX!
OBELIX!
BOOHOO! BOOHOO! I SHOULDN'T HAVE SAID WHAT I SAID!
I SHOULDN'T HAVE CALLED YOU A GREEDY PIG!
HOWWWL!
COME ON, LET'S HAVE A BEER!
SMASHING!
YAP! YAP!
HM! THEY'RE CELEBRATING SOMETHING IN THERE!
I'M WORRIED, OBELIX. EVERYONE IN THE VILLAGE IS SO JUMPY. THINGS COULD TAKE A TURN FOR THE WORSE...
SCRUNCH! SCRUNCH!
THEY COULD INDEED... VITALSTATISTIX HAS JUST GIVEN HIS OWN ACCOUNT OF RECENT EVENTS, STRESSING THE BONDS OF FRIENDSHIP BETWEEN ASTERIX AND THE MYSTERIOUS ROMAN.
I DON'T GO CHASING AFTER HONOURS; I DON'T INVITE ALL AND SUNDRY HOME, NOT EVEN ROMANS! I COULD BE A ROMAN SENATOR IF I WANTED TO, BUT YOU KNOW ME, MY LOVE...
JUST WAIT TILL MY FRIENDS HEAR ABOUT THIS! IT SO HAPPENS I'VE INVITED THEM FOR A CUP OF GOAT'S MILK* TO TALK ABOUT THIS BUSINESS!
* TEA, THOUGH WELL KNOWN IN THE VILLAGE, IS NOT IN WIDESPREAD USE.

I HOPE I'M NOT LATE?
OF COURSE NOT.
NOT TOO MUCH, JUST A LITTLE!
OH, IT'S ONLY MILK, SUGAR, EGGS, FLOUR AND BOAR FAT – NOT AT ALL FATTENING.
IMPEDIMENTA, ABOUT THIS MORNING... IT WAS ONLY A BIT OF FUN... A JOKE.
OF COURSE! LET'S TALK ABOUT MORE IMPORTANT THINGS...
MY HUSBAND THE CHIEF – JULIUS CAESAR NOMINATED HIM A SENATOR, BUT HE REFUSED, OF COURSE – WELL, HE'S GIVING A GREAT DEAL OF THOUGHT TO ASTERIX AND HIS FRIENDSHIP WITH THAT ROMAN.
YES, MY HUSBAND FULLIAUTOMATIX TOLD ME THEY WERE HAVING A GOOD TIME. HE HEARD LAUGHTER AND SINGING. THEY SEEMED TO HAVE BEEN DRINKING!
HOW DREADFUL! YOU KNOW, I'VE ALWAYS HAD MY DOUBTS ABOUT ASTERIX. A MAN OF HIS AGE, AND STILL A BACHELOR...
HOW OLD IS HE EXACTLY?
GOODNESS KNOWS! MY HUSBAND GERIATRIX SAYS HE'S NOT SO YOUNG AS HE LOOKS!
MMMM... AND HIS FRIEND OBELIX? DO YOU THINK HE'S A GOOD INFLUENCE? ALL THAT GREEDY PIG THINKS OF IS HIS FOOD!
THE TROUBLE IS THAT ASTERIX IS OUR DRUID GETAFIX'S FAVOURITE, AND HE KNOWS A LOT OF SECRETS...
THE SECRET OF THE MAGIC POTION, FOR EXAMPLE?
MY LIPS ARE SEALED.
AND SOON AFTERWARDS...
...SO ASTERIX HAS SOLD THE SECRET OF THE MAGIC POTION TO THE ROMANS? THESE YOUNG PEOPLE! I ASK YOU!

SO THAT'S IT – MY WIFE WAS VISITING THE SENATOR'S WIFE, AND SHE FOUND OUT THAT ASTERIX HAD SOLD THE SECRET OF THE MAGIC POTION TO THE ROMANS.
HE GOT A VASE FULL OF PRECIOUS STONES FOR IT.
THAT'S TERRIBLE! THE ROMANS WILL MASSACRE US!
COT!
HUH! I DON'T NEED ANY MAGIC POTION! I DIDN'T HAVE ANY AT GERGOVIA!
YOU CAN'T CONVINCE ME THAT ASTERIX HAS DONE A THING LIKE THAT. I SHOULD LIKE SOME PROOF.
DO YOU THINK IT'S NORMAL FOR THAT ROMAN TO BE GIVING ASTERIX PRESENTS?
WELL, NO...
OH, TAKE NO NOTICE OF HIM! UNHYGIENIX IS A SHOPKEEPER, SO SELLING FISH OR POTIONS, IT'S ALL THE SAME TO HIM!
SAY THAT AGAIN?
YOU HEARD!
16A
PAFF!
ASTERIX IS A TRAITOR!
NO, HE ISN'T!
YES, HE IS!
LOOK OUT! HERE HE COMES! ACT NORMAL! LET'S MAKE OUT WE'RE DOING NOTHING!
TRA LA LA!
SMACK!
?
16B

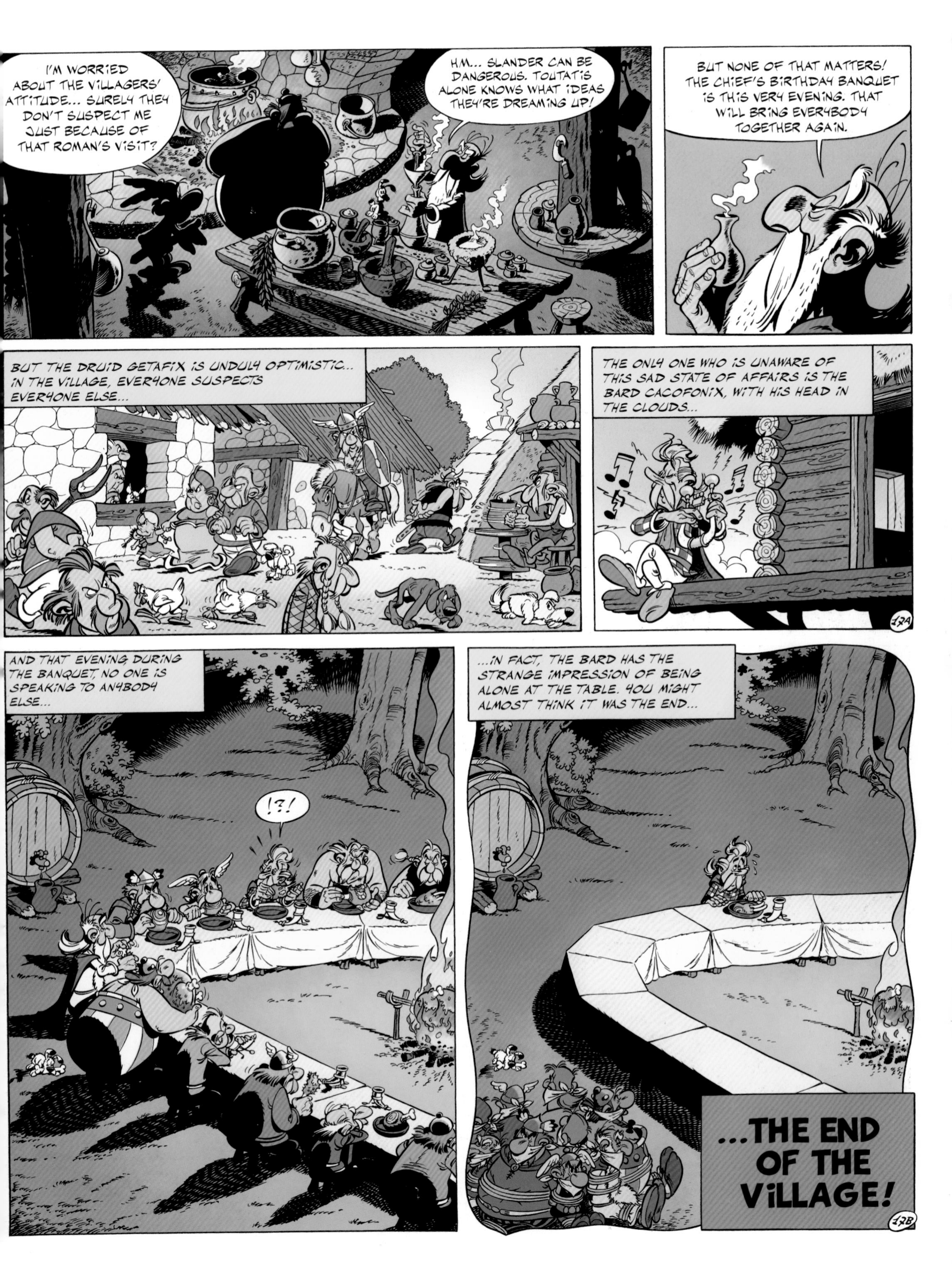
I'M WORRIED ABOUT THE VILLAGERS' ATTITUDE... SURELY THEY DON'T SUSPECT ME JUST BECAUSE OF THAT ROMAN'S VISIT?
HM... SLANDER CAN BE DANGEROUS. TOUTATIS ALONE KNOWS WHAT IDEAS THEY'RE DREAMING UP!
BUT NONE OF THAT MATTERS! THE CHIEF'S BIRTHDAY BANQUET IS THIS VERY EVENING. THAT WILL BRING EVERYBODY TOGETHER AGAIN.
BUT THE DRUID GETAFIX IS UNDULY OPTIMISTIC... IN THE VILLAGE, EVERYONE SUSPECTS EVERYONE ELSE...
THE ONLY ONE WHO IS UNAWARE OF THIS SAD STATE OF AFFAIRS IS THE BARD CACOFONIX, WITH HIS HEAD IN THE CLOUDS...
17A
AND THAT EVENING DURING THE BANQUET, NO ONE IS SPEAKING TO ANYBODY ELSE...
!?!
...IN FACT, THE BARD HAS THE STRANGE IMPRESSION OF BEING ALONE AT THE TABLE. YOU MIGHT ALMOST THINK IT WAS THE END...
...THE END OF THE VILLAGE!
17B

NEXT DAY, A ROMAN PATROL IS SCOUTING AROUND IN THE FOREST, TAKING NO CHANCES...
FOOTSTEPS!
LET'S HIDE IN THAT TREE OVER THERE!
OUCH! LET'S USE A DIFFERENT TREE!
THERE'S NO TIME! SSH!
IT'S VERY KIND OF YOU TO COME AND HELP ME CHECK MY SNARES, FULLIAUTOMATIX!
I WANTED A QUIET WORD WITH YOU, AWAY FROM THE OTHERS...
OUCH!
SSH! OOH!
YOU'RE AN EXPERIENCED CHAP, GERIATRIX... IF THE ROMANS DO HAVE THE MAGIC POTION, IT'S VERY SERIOUS... MY WIFE THINKS THE TIME HAS COME TO LEAVE THE DISTRICT.
HUH! THE ROMANS DON'T SCARE ME WITH THEIR MAGIC POTION. I'M READY TO FIGHT AGAIN, AS WE DID AT GERGOVIA!
18A
HAVE WE GOT THE MAGIC POTION?
SURELY WE'D KNOW!
BY THE WAY, BOYS, NOW THE GAULS HAVE GONE, SHALL WE GET DOWN FROM THIS TREE?
YES, BECAUSE OF THE WASPS!
BZZZZZZZZZZZZZZZZZZ
BACK AT AQUARIUM...
WE'VE GOT THE MAGIC POTION!
WE'VE GOT THE MAGIC POTION!!
???
CLINK!
18B

WHAT'S GOING ON HERE, BY JUPITER?
WE'VE FOUND OUT WE'VE GOT THE SECRET OF THE MAGIC POTION...
ALL THE LADS ARE ASKING WHY YOU DON'T GIVE US ANY, INSTEAD OF LETTING US GET BASHED ABOUT BY THOSE GAULISH NUTS!
TEEHEE! YOUR MAGIC POTION IS ME!
?
A CAULDRON, QUICK! GET HIM STEWED!
NO THANKS! I'M NOT EATING THAT, I NEVER TOUCH IT!
SIMMER DOWN! EVERYTHING IS GOING ACCORDING TO PLAN!
WE'LL SPREAD IT ABOUT THAT WE DO HAVE THE MAGIC POTION, AND I PROMISE YOU THE GAULS WILL SOON SPLIT UP AND GO AWAY.
WE ARE SOLDIERS! WE DON'T LIKE THE DEVIOUS WAYS OF CIVIL SERVANTS! WE PREFER HONOURABLE BATTLES, THE CLASH OF ARMS, THE CLARION CALL OF BUCINAS...
...BLOOD, TOIL, TEARS AND...
RIGHT, WHAT DO WE DO, CONVOLVULUS?
?!?
COME WITH ME. I'LL TELL YOU MY PLANS.

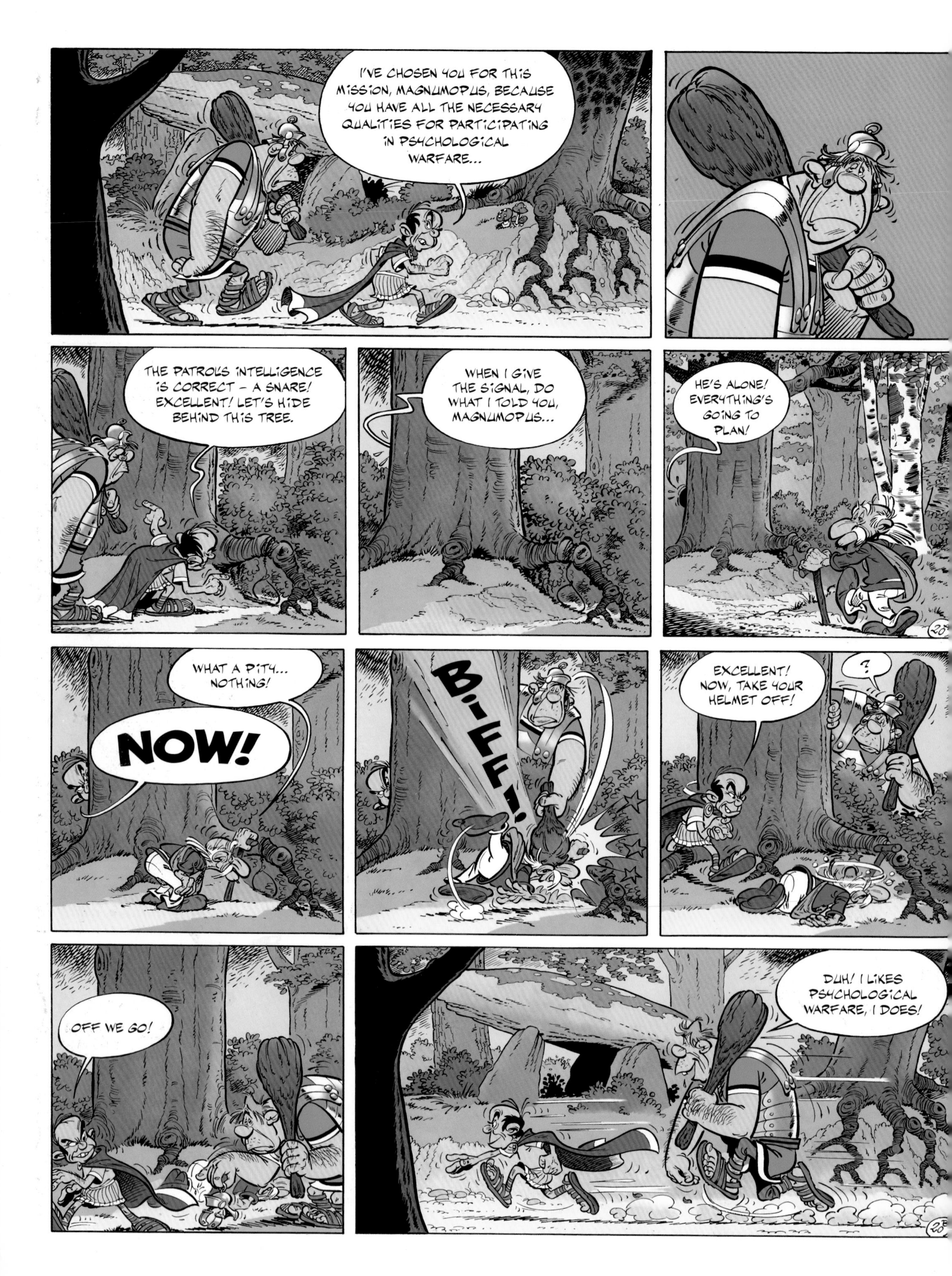
I'VE CHOSEN YOU FOR THIS MISSION, MAGNUMOPUS, BECAUSE YOU HAVE ALL THE NECESSARY QUALITIES FOR PARTICIPATING IN PSYCHOLOGICAL WARFARE...
THE PATROL'S INTELLIGENCE IS CORRECT – A SNARE! EXCELLENT! LET'S HIDE BEHIND THIS TREE.
WHEN I GIVE THE SIGNAL, DO WHAT I TOLD YOU, MAGNUMOPUS...
HE'S ALONE! EVERYTHING'S GOING TO PLAN!
WHAT A PITY... NOTHING!
NOW!
BIFF!
EXCELLENT! NOW, TAKE YOUR HELMET OFF!
?
OFF WE GO!
DUH! I LIKES PSYCHOLOGICAL WARFARE, I DOES!

ALESIA! IT'S ALESIA ALL OVER AGAIN!
?
?
?
?
?
?
?
?
THEY'VE GOT THE MAGIC POTION!
THE ROMANS ATTACKED ME! THEY'VE GOT SUPER-HUMAN STRENGTH! I WASN'T BEATEN EASILY, AND I MANAGED TO SNATCH THIS TROPHY. ONLY THE MAGIC POTION COULD HAVE MADE THEM STRONG ENOUGH TO OVERCOME ME!
THAT PROVES IT! THEY'VE GOT THE POTION!
OUT OF THE QUESTION! ONLY OUR DRUID KNOWS ITS SECRET!
HE'S NOT THE ONLY ONE NOW!
HAVE YOU ALL GONE MAD, BY TOUTATIS? YOU DON'T NEED MAGIC POTION TO KNOCK GERIATRIX OUT!
WHAT'S THAT?
ALL THE SAME, A ROMAN WOULD HAVE TO BE PRETTY SURE OF HIMSELF TO ATTACK EVEN THIS OLD RELIC!
LOOK HERE...
?
AND LOOK AT THAT TINY LITTLE HELMET! THE LEGIONARY WHO WORE IT MUST HAVE BEEN A PROPER TITCH! WE ALWAYS KNEW GERIATRIX HAD SMALL LATIN...
?
...BUT SURELY EVEN GERIATRIX COULD HAVE MASTERED ANY LATIN THAT SMALL!
AND YOU KNOW WHAT GERIATRIX SAYS TO YOU?!?
WE MUST FIND OUT FOR SURE WHETHER THE ROMANS HAVE THE MAGIC POTION.
I'LL GO AND ASK THEM IF YOU LIKE.
NO, NOT YOU. UNHYGIENIX AND FULLIAUTOMATIX, YOU GO!

WHY DIDN'T HE WANT ME TO GO?
ASTERIX, I THINK THAT WE SHALL SOON HAVE TO TEACH OUR FRIENDS A LITTLE LESSON.
SO DO I!
MEANWHILE, AT AQUARIUM...
COME ALONG, PLATYPUS! WE'VE GOT WORK TO DO!
I DIDN'T JOIN UP TO WORK! TALK ABOUT THE CONSTANT SERVICE OF THE ANTIQUE WORLD! EVER SINCE WE'VE HAD CIVIL SERVANTS IN CHARGE...
?
PAF!
WHAT ARE YOU DOING, YOU IDIOT?
DUH! I'M TELLING THEM ABOUT PSYCHOLOGICAL WARFARE.
PAF!
PSYCHOLOGICAL WARFARE? WHAT'S THIS NEWFANGLED NOTION?
PAF!
THIS ISN'T THE MOMENT TO FOOL ABOUT! BRING ALL THOSE IDIOTS ROUND AND BOIL ME UP A BIG CAULDRON OF WATER!
MEANWHILE, IN ANOTHER PART OF THE FOREST...
IF THE ROMANS REALLY DO HAVE THE MAGIC POTION, THIS COULD BE A DANGEROUS MISSION, AND THE WAY YOU SMELL OF FISH, WE RUN CONSIDERABLE RISK OF DETECTION!
YOU'RE BEGINNING TO GET ON MY NERVES, FULLIAUTOMATIX!
I WONDER WHAT'S UP, CHAPS? DO YOU THINK IT'S A RED HERRING?

TRY NOT TO SMELL!
BY TOUTATIS!
THEY HAVE GOT IT!
LET'S HAVE A LOOK!
FUNNY THING... SNIFF! ... I SMELL SOMETHING FISHY.
EXCELLENT! IT MUST BE THE GAULS SPYING ON US...
HOMUNCULUS! MAGNUMOPUS! CARRY OUT OUR PLAN!
AHA! NOW TO FIND OUT IF THIS MAGIC POTION REALLY WORKS!
BIFF!
BOOOOM!
THEY'VE GOT IT! THEY'VE GOT IT!
WE MUST WARN THE OTHERS!
NO, IT ISN'T: IT'S A FLYING FISH!

RIGHT. WE CAN STOP NOW. THEY SHOULD HAVE GONE.
STOP?
BUT WE HAVEN'T HAD OUR MAGIC POTION YET!
IT'S NOT FAIR!
WE'VE GOT A RIGHT TO HAVE OUR MAGIC POTION!
?
BUT IT ISN'T MAGIC POTION! IT'S ONLY HOT WATER!
WHAT D'YOU MEAN, IT ISN'T MAGIC POTION? WHAT ABOUT HIM, THEN?
BUT I EXPLAINED IT ALL TO YOU! WE'RE JUST PRETENDING!
CLONK!
OH, SO IT ISN'T MAGIC POTION, EH? WHAT ABOUT THAT, THEN? I'VE KNOCKED OUT THE MAN WHO KNOCKED OUT MAGNUMOPUS!
BUT MAGNUMOPUS ISN'T REALLY KNOCKED OUT!
GET UP AND SHOW HIM, MAGNUMOPUS.
HAVE A GO WITH ME, MAGNUMOPUS?
CLONK!
DUH! THIS PSYCHOLOGICAL WARFARE IS GOOD STUFF!
PAF!
YOUR PLANS ARE TOO COMPLICATED, CONVOLVULUS... I DON'T KNOW WHERE WE ARE NOW MYSELF.. SO WHO **HAS** GOT THE MAGIC POTION?
SCRATCH! SCRATCH!

THEY'VE GOT iT!
THE ROMANS HAVE GOT THE MAGiC POTiON! WE SAW THEM!
THAT'S RiDiCULOUS! HOW COULD THEY HAVE MANAGED TO FiND OUT THE SECRET?
PUFF! PUFF!
WE'VE BEEN SEEiNG A LOT OF ROMANS AROUND THE ViLLAGE LATELY.
ARE YOU ACCUSiNG ME OF GiViNG THE ROMANS THE SECRET OF THE MAGiC POTiON?
AND HOW ABOUT YOU, ViTALSTATiSTiX? ARE YOU ACCUSiNG ME OF TELLiNG ASTERiX THE SECRET – THE SECRET THAT MAY ONLY BE HANDED DOWN FROM DRUiD TO DRUiD, BY WORD OF MOUTH?
ER... WELL...
ALL RiGHT. I GET THE MESSAGE. I'M LEAViNG THE ViLLAGE.
ME TOO.
WELL, THEN, ME TOO.
WOOF
25A
BUT DRUiD... iF YOU WALK OUT ON US WE WON'T HAVE ANY MAGiC POTiON!
ALL YOU HAD TO DO WAS FALL iN iT WHEN YOU WERE BABiES!
SO THERE!
I WONDER iF WE MAY JUST POSSiBLY HAVE DONE A SiLLY THiNG, BOYS...
YOU SHOULD HAVE STOPPED THEM, SENATOR.
STOP CALLiNG ME SENATOR, iDiOT! GET OUT OF MY SiGHT!
I FEEL VERY LOW...
POTOP! POTOP!
25B

ALL THE SAME, IT'S A PITY WE'RE LEAVING. NOW THE ROMANS HAVE GOT THE MAGIC POTION IT'LL BE MORE FUN.
THEY HAVEN'T GOT THE MAGIC POTION!
WHO HAS GOT THE MAGIC POTION, THEN?
DON'T LET IT BOTHER YOU, OBELIX.
NO ONE EVER EXPLAINS ANYTHING TO ME! THEY JUST KEEP ME AROUND BECAUSE I'M ORNAMENTAL!
POF!
GOOD MORNING, LEGIONARY. WE COME IN PEACE. WE WANT TO SEE THAT NEW ROMAN...
CONVOLVULUS, THE CIVIL SERVANT? THIRD TENT ON THE LEFT.
26
WHAT HAVE YOU GOT ON YOUR HEAD?
THEY'VE BEEN PRACTISING PSYCHOLOGY ON ME.
YOU AND DOGMATIX WAIT FOR US HERE, OBELIX.
RIGHT.
HEY!
QUID?
SNAP!
THERE'S SOMETHING I'D LIKE TO CHECK UP ON, IF YOU DON'T MIND...
CARRY ON.
PLAFF!
26B

YOU!?
YES, US. WE'VE COME TO TELL YOU THAT YOU'VE WON!
YOU'VE SUCCEEDED IN SOWING DISCORD IN OUR VILLAGE BY SPREADING LIES AND SLANDER.
WH... WHAT ARE YOU GOING TO DO TO ME?
NOTHING. WE'VE JUST COME TO TELL YOU WE DESPISE YOU. WE'RE NOT INTERESTED IN YOU OR THE VILLAGERS WHO WERE SO READY TO BELIEVE YOUR LIES.
WE'RE LEAVING THESE PARTS, ALONG WITH OBELIX AND THE MAGIC POTION!
??
I CHECKED UP ON IT! THEY HAVEN'T GOT THE MAGIC POTION. THEY'RE AS SOFT AS EVER.
LET'S GET OUT OF THIS CAMP.
!
DID YOU SEE THAT, DOGMATIX? NO ONE'S GOT THE MAGIC POTION NOW, AND THEY'RE LAUGHING!
WE CAN SEE EVERYTHING THAT GOES ON IN THE CAMP FROM OUR VANTAGE POINT IN THIS TREE.

I'VE DONE IT! IT WORKED! THE DRUID, THE DWARF AND THE MONSTER HAVE LEFT THE VILLAGE!
EXPLAIN YOURSELF, CONVOLVULUS. YOU'RE MAKING LESS SENSE ALL THE TIME.
NOW THAT THOSE THREE GAULS HAVE GONE, THE OTHERS WILL BE HARMLESS. NO MORE DRUID, NO MORE MAGIC POTION!
I GET IT!
SOUND THE BUCINAS AND TRUMPETS! TO ARMS! EVERYONE FALL IN! ALL ABLE-BODIED PERSONNEL TO REVIVE THOSE WHO WERE BRAIN-WASHED!
TANTANTARA TARAA!
28A
?!?
AND WHAT, MAY I ASK, IS THAT?
WELL, SINCE THERE ARE SOME WHO SAY WE HAVEN'T GOT THE MAGIC POTION, WE THOUGHT PSYCHOLOGICAL WAR...
THAT WILL DO! YOU'RE IN THE ROMAN ARMY NOW!
STAND TO ATTENTION! NO FALLING OUT OF LINE! YOU WILL MASSACRE ACCORDING TO THE RULES! I DON'T WANT ANY FANCY NOTIONS HERE! GO AND GET YOUR WEAPONS!
28B

SOON AFTERWARDS...
RIGHT! LEGIONARIES, WE ARE ABOUT TO ATTACK THE GAULISH VILLAGE AND WIPE IT OFF THE FACE OF THE ROMAN EARTH! THE GAULS HAVEN'T GOT ANY MORE MAGIC POTION, AND...
BUT... ER... HAVE WE GOT THE MAGIC POTION, THEN?
YES, OF COURSE WE HAVE!
NO, OF COURSE WE HAVEN'T!
YES, WE HAVE!
I TELL YOU WE HAVEN'T!
BUT HOMUNCULUS...
LOOK, JOKING APART, HAVE WE GOT IT OR HAVE WE NOT?
LISTEN! NO ONE'S GOT THE MAGIC POTION, BUT WE OUTNUMBER THE GAULS TWENTY TO ONE! WE SHALL WIN EASILY, AND CAESAR WILL REWARD US!
SO... UP, LEGIONARIES, AND AT 'EM!
AVE CAESAR!
I SEE THAT MIXING WITH US HAS MADE YOU A CUNNING STRATEGIST!
TANTANTARA! TARAA! BONG! BONG!
IT'S WORKING LIKE A CHARM! THEY'VE LEFT THE CAMP! OFF WE GO!

THEY HAVEN'T EVEN LEFT A SENTRY!
WHAT ARE WE GOING TO DO IN THIS CAMP IF THERE AREN'T ANY ROMANS LEFT?
AHA! THERE'S THEIR CAULDRON OF SO-CALLED MAGIC POTION!
YOU'RE GOING TO CARRY IT, OBELIX, WITHOUT SPILLING A DROP.
IS THIS MAGIC POTION?
MY DEAR OBELIX, IF YOU DRANK IT IT WOULDN'T HAVE ANY EFFECT ON YOU AT ALL.
OH, THEN IT IS MAGIC POTION. MAGIC POTION NEVER DOES HAVE ANY EFFECT ON ME AT ALL.
?
SOMETIMES HE MAKES ME WONDER IF I KNOW WHAT I MEAN MYSELF!
LET'S NOT WASTE TIME. WE HAVE TO REACH THE VILLAGE BEFORE THE ROMANS.
SURE ENOUGH, THE LEGIONARIES ARE PASSING THROUGH THE FOREST IN THE DIRECTION OF THE VILLAGE...
I SAY, THE LADS WANT TO KNOW HOW THE LOOT IS GOING TO BE SHARED OUT THIS TIME, BECAUSE AT MUNDA...
WELL, WHAT ABOUT MUNDA? WHAT HAPPENED AT MUNDA?
THE LOOT WAS PERFECTLY FAIRLY DISTRIBUTED... LET'S SEE, THERE WERE THOSE TWELVE VALUABLE VASES...
LET'S NOT COUNT ON VALUABLE VASES... YOU MIGHT GET A NASTY JAR!
SURE ENOUGH, IN THE VILLAGE, THE GAULS ARE GETTING READY TO PROVE THAT THEY ARE NOT BY ANY MEANS OLD CROCKS...
WITH OR WITHOUT POTION, WE'LL SHOW THEM WHO WE ARE!
WE'D BETTER NOT SHOW THEM HOW MANY WE ARE, THAT'S ALL!

THERE THEY ARE!
WE MUST REACH THE VILLAGE AHEAD OF THEM! TAKE A GOOD SWIG OF MAGIC POTION, ASTERIX!
NO, NO, NOT THAT ONE, OBELIX!
GLUG! GLUG! GLUG!
OUCH! THEY'RE ATTACKING US IN THE REAR!
BUT... BUT WE'RE THE REAR!
TCHAPATRAC!
OUR REAR IS BEING ATTACKED!
OUR REAR IS BEING ATTACKED! PASS IT ON!!!
THIS IS A PRETTY PASS!
BUT SOMEONE MUST HAVE SOLD IT...
THE REAR IS BEING ATTACKED!
WHAT?
?!
CLONK!

ASTERIX, OBELIX AND GETAFIX ARE COMING BACK!!!
QUICK, YOU TWO! GO AND OPEN THE GATES!
RIGHT, CHIEF!
MIND THE SHIELD, WILL YOU, CHIEF?
SHUT THE GATES!
MEANWHILE...
WHAT HAPPENED?
O CENTURION PLATYPUS, I HAVE ENDANGERED MY LIFE TO BRING YOU THIS REPORT! THE REAR WAS TREACHEROUSLY ATTACKED, AND SURRENDERED ONLY AFTER A TERRIBLE STRUGGLE!
IDIOT! OWING TO THE FAILURE OF THE REAR TO BACK US UP, THE ORDER OF MARCH HAS BEEN TURNED BACK TO FRONT! NOW GET BACK TO THE FRONT!
?!
DID YOU BY ANY CHANCE FAIL TO UNDERSTAND ME?
WELL, TO BE HONEST...
GET ON WITH IT!!!
CALM DOWN... THINGS AREN'T TURNING OUT QUITE AS EXPECTED... THE GAULS HAVE GONE BACK TO THE VILLAGE WITH OUR MAGIC POTION...
BUT IT ISN'T THE REAL MAGIC POTION... OR IF IT IS, I'M DROPPING THE WHOLE AFFAIR ON THE GROUNDS OF TOTAL INCOMPREHENSIBILITY!

GOOD OF YOU TO COME BACK... GETAFIX, I WONDER IF I COULD POSSIBLY ASK YOU TO MAKE A LITTLE MAGIC POTION...
MAGIC POTION? HERE YOU ARE! WE'VE BEEN TO THE ROMAN CAMP TO GET IT.
THE ROMAN CAMP?
THAT'S RIGHT. FULLIAUTOMATIX AND UNHYGIENIX TOLD YOU IT WAS MAGIC POTION – THEY SAW THE ROMANS DRINKING IT.
COME ON, THEN, HAVE SOME! WHO'S FIRST?
GLUG! GLUG! GLUG!
IT DOESN'T TASTE OF ANYTHING MUCH.
IT MAY WORK... TRY UPROOTING THAT TREE.
GNGNGN!
GIVE HIM A HAND, ASTERIX!
WITH PLEASURE, O DRUID!
GASP! GASP! GASP!
CRAAASH!
OIII! I'M NOT BOTHERING YOU, SO KINDLY LET ME COMPOSE MY BALLADS IN PEACE!!!
THAT'S THE POTION WE NEED, GETAFIX.
OH, SO YOU DON'T THINK THE ROMANS' POTION IS THE SAME AS MINE, VITALSTATISTIX?

THERE'S NOT A MOMENT TO BE LOST! THE GAULS KNOW THAT OUR POTION IS NO GOOD. THEIR DRUID IS GOING TO MAKE THEM SOME OF THE REAL STUFF! WE MUST ATTACK AT ONCE. IT'S OUR ONLY CHANCE!
ATTA...!?
WHERE'S THAT LOT GONE?
THE VANGUARD WENT TO HELP THE REAR, AND I STAYED AT THE FRONT BACK HERE, BECAUSE AFTER ALL PSYCHOLOGICAL WARFARE...
GO AND FIND ME ALL THOSE IDIOTS, IDIOT!
MEANWHILE...
ALL RIGHT, SO WE BEHAVED BADLY. WE BELIEVED THE SLANDERS THAT ROMAN SPREAD, AND WE WERE WRONG... YOU WOULDN'T LET US DOWN NOW, WOULD YOU?
NEVER MIND! IT'LL BE LIKE GERGOVIA! WE DON'T NEED ANY POTION! LET'S GO!
HE'S RIGHT! LET'S GO!
I'M COMING TOO!
I DON'T KNOW WHERE YOU'RE GOING, BUT I'M GOING WITH YOU!
WE'LL ALL GO!
BIFF!
THIS IS MORE LIKE YOU! ABSOLUTELY CRAZY, BUT UNITED ONCE AGAIN. NOW I'LL MAKE YOU SOME MAGIC POTION! REAL MAGIC POTION!
BUT THAT WILL TAKE TIME, AND THE ROMANS...
WELL, YOU AND OBELIX HOLD THE ROMANS OFF!

DO YOU GET IT, OBELIX? WE MUST HOLD THEM OFF UNTIL OUR DRUID HAS FINISHED MAKING THE MAGIC POTION.
I DON'T REALLY GET ANYTHING, BUT I'M WITH YOU ALL THE WAY!
SURRENDER, GAULS!
MAY I?
BY ALL MEANS.
BIFF!
CRASH!
PLONK!
KERPLONK!
BIFF!
BIFF!
RETIRE!
ASTERIX, WE MUST PRESS THEM TO STAY! IF THEY GO AWAY WE CAN'T HOLD THEM OFF!
NO, IT'S A PITY THE ROMAN TROOPS HAVE SUCH RETIRING DISPOSITIONS.
A WHOLE ARMY PUT TO FLIGHT BY TWO BARBARIANS. OH, WON'T CAESAR BE PLEASED WHEN I TELL HIM ABOUT THIS!
THERE ISN'T ANYTHING TO TELL. THIS IS A STRATEGIC WITHDRAWAL. I'M GOING TO ASK THE OTHER GARRISONS TO BRING UP REINFORCEMENTS AND TAKE THEM IN THE REAR. WE SHALL CRUSH THEM BY SHEER WEIGHT OF NUMBERS!
OF COURSE, THERE ARE TWO OF THEM, AND WE'RE ONLY ONE GARRISON.
TAKE THESE MESSAGES TO LAUDANUM, TOTORUM AND COMPENDIUM. HURRY!
SURE ENOUGH, TIME IS RUNNING OUT FOR THE ROMANS...
JUST LET IT SIMMER FOR A FEW MORE MINUTES...

ALL I NEED IS A SPRIG OF MISTLETOE!
BUT THERE ISN'T ANY MISTLETOE LEFT IN THE VILLAGE! WE'LL HAVE TO GO AND LOOK FOR SOME IN THE FOREST!
OBELIX, MY DEAR FELLOW, TAKE MY SICKLE AND GO AND FIND ME A BIT OF MISTLETOE ON THOSE TREES OVER THERE!
?
THEY TOLD ME I WAS GOING TO HOLD OFF THE ROMANS, AND NOW THEY SEND ME OUT FOR VEGETABLES...
THEY'RE COUNTER-ATTACKING! TO ARMS!
IT'S NOT MY JOB TO RUN ERRANDS!
CLONK!
YOU ROMANS ARE CRAZY! WHEN WE'RE LOOKING FOR A FIGHT...
BIFF!
...YOU'RE NEVER AROUND...
SBLOING!
BUT I'M NOT HERE FOR THE FIGHTING JUST NOW, SO KINDLY LET ME RUN MY ERRANDS IN PEACE.
?
WHAT'S HE AFTER UP THERE?
SPLONG!
OOF! I WAS AFRAID IT WAS OBSOLETE!

?
!
ASTERIX! ASTERIX! THERE ARE MASSES OF ROMANS, COMING FROM ALL OVER THE PLACE!
OH, SO THAT'S WHY THEY STOPPED ATTACKING... THEY WERE WAITING FOR REINFORCEMENTS!
THE ROMAN GARRISONS ARE ALL MARCHING ON US!
IT'S NEARLY READY. THEY'LL GET A TASTE OF THEIR OWN MEDICINE.
AVE PLATYPUS! THE GARRISON OF TOTORUM...
...AND THE GARRISON OF LAUDANUM...
...AND THE GARRISON OF COMPENDIUM ARE HERE IN RESPONSE TO YOUR REQUEST!
AVE, FRIENDS! RIGHT, THEN...
ATTACK!
COME AND GET IT!
SOON AFTERWARDS...
HAS EVERYONE HAD HIS PORTION OF POTION? RIGHT, THEN...
ATTACK!

THE BATTLE OF THE ViLLAGE

Only a panoramic view can do justice to the complex nature of this terrible battle, in which a small village of indomitable Gauls comes to grips with the garrisons of the fortified Roman camps of Aquarium, Totorum, Laudanum and Compendium.

1 Indomitable little Gaulish village.
2 Garrison of Aquarium (Roman camp).
3 Garrison of Roman camp of Totorum.
4 Garrison of Roman camp of Laudanum.
5 Garrison of Roman camp of Compendium.
6, 7, 8, 9 Gauls pouring out of the village any old how, without any plan of battle.
10 Druid Getafix awaiting the outcome of the battle beside his cauldron, now empty.
11 Bard Cacofonix asking the druid what it's all about, and what, might he ask, is going on?
12 Pirate ship sunk by Gauls pouring out at (**8**) full of enthusiasm, discovering on arrival at the beach that there are no Romans available, and deciding not to waste their time anyway, by Toutatis.
13 Obelix, menhir delivery man, trying to keep back the Gauls while explaining to them that he got there first, he didn't ring for anyone, he would like to be left alone with his own Romans and they don't want to be disturbed.
14 Fulliautomatix, village blacksmith, catching sight of an old friend.
15 Unhygienix, village fishmonger, friend of the afore-mentioned.
16 Point of intersection of the two friends.
17 Geriatrix, village elder, engaged in single combat with Magnumopus, Roman legionary.
18 Vitalstatistix, chief of the Gaulish village, badly let down by his shield-bearers, who have jumped the fence without bothering to see that he kept his balance. He feels understandably downcast for a few moments.

THE BATTLE, ALTHOUGH VIOLENT, IS OF SHORT DURATION, AND THE VICTORS ARE LEFT IN POSSESSION OF THE BATTLEFIELD, THEIR ARMS FULL OF TROPHIES...
TEEHEEHEE!
SLAP! SLAP!
I CALL THAT BATTLE A REAL SUCCESS; IT WAS A GREAT CRUSH!
YES, BUT THERE'S STILL SOMETHING WE HAVE TO DO. CALL THE OTHERS!
A LITTLE FARTHER AWAY...
OH, SO THERE YOU ARE. YOU AND YOUR TROUBLEMAKING! BRAVO! OH, VERY WELL DONE! WE WERE GOING ALONG QUIETLY AS USUAL, THE GAULS WERE MINDING THEIR OWN BUSINESS, AND NOW WE'VE SUFFERED A DEFEAT, THANKS TO YOU!
AS FOR ME, I DID WHAT I HAD TO DO... IT WAS YOU OTHERS WHO...
HEY!
39A
!!!
ALL RIGHT, I'M GOING... I'M NOT NEEDED HERE ANY MORE...
LEGIONARIES! ARREST THAT PERSON!
39B

THANKS VERY MUCH, CONVOLVULUS!
?
I BEG YOUR PARDON?
YOU DID WELL! WE'RE PLEASED WITH YOU. YOU KEPT YOUR WORD!
YOU'LL ALWAYS FIND A WELCOME IN OUR VILLAGE, CONVOLVULUS!
AND HERE'S A LITTLE SOUVENIR OVER AND ABOVE THE PRICE WE SETTLED...
LONG LIVE CONVOLVULUS!
UP WITH CONVOLVULUS!
UP WITH OUR OLD PAL!
BUT... BUT...
HA! NOW I SEE IT ALL! YOU WERE ON THEIR SIDE ALL THE TIME! THAT EXPLAINS OUR DEFEAT!
I NEVER! IT'S A SLANDER! YOU CAN'T BELIEVE SUCH WICKED LIES!
OH, CAN'T WE JUST!!!
CRASH!
PUT HIM IN CHAINS! WE'LL BE SENDING HIM BACK TO ROME TO CAESAR, CHARGED WITH HIGH TREASON!
BUT WE NEED NOT BE UNDULY WORRIED ABOUT THE TROUBLEMAKER: CONVOLVULUS WILL WRIGGLE HIS WAY OUT OF ANYTHING AND EVEN ON BOARD THE GALLEY WHICH IS TAKING HIM BACK TO ROME, HE DOES NOT FEEL ALONE... SLANDER, JEALOUSY AND CALUMNY HAVE EMBARKED WITH HIM!
I SAID TO PORT!
STOP SHOVING YOUR OAR IN, CAPTAIN – WE ALL KNOW THE SORT OF PULL YOU USED TO GET YOUR JOB!

WE'VE BEHAVED BADLY TOWARDS YOU, ASTERIX; OUR FRIENDSHIP SHOULD HAVE BEEN PROOF AGAINST ANY SLANDERS. YOU AND GETAFIX AND OBELIX HAVE TAUGHT US A LESSON, AND YOU HAVE SAVED OUR VILLAGE BY BANISHING DISCORD FROM IT...
ASTERIX, WE BOW TO YOU!
NO, I DO THE BOWING, NOT YOU!!!!
SOMETIMES HE ACTS IN THE MOST UNBALANCED WAY!
IF HE CARRIES ON LIKE THIS WE'LL LET HIM DOWN ONE OF THESE DAYS!
FORGIVE US, ASTERIX!
LET BYGONES BE BYGONES! WE'LL ORGANIZE A BIRTHDAY FEAST FOR OUR CHIEF! A REAL ONE, NOT A FLOP LIKE LAST TIME!
BRAVO, BY TOUTATIS!
I'M GOING TO GIVE HIM ANOTHER MENHIR!
I'M GOING TO GIVE HIM A SWORD!
I CAUGHT A GOOD FISH LAST WEEK. IT'LL BE JUST WHAT HE WANTED!
IT WILL BE A LOVELY SURPRISE FOR THE CHIEF!
MEANWHILE...
WHAT A WONDERFUL SURPRISE! MY DEAR FRIENDS, I AM AT A LOSS FOR WORDS...
I'M GLAD WE'RE ALL FRIENDS AGAIN!
ALL THE SAME, I'D LIKE TO KNOW IF THEY REALLY ARE CURED.
I MUST SAY, IT WOULD BE INTERESTING TO FIND OUT... AND IT'S ABOUT TIME YOU GOT A BIT OF YOUR OWN BACK.

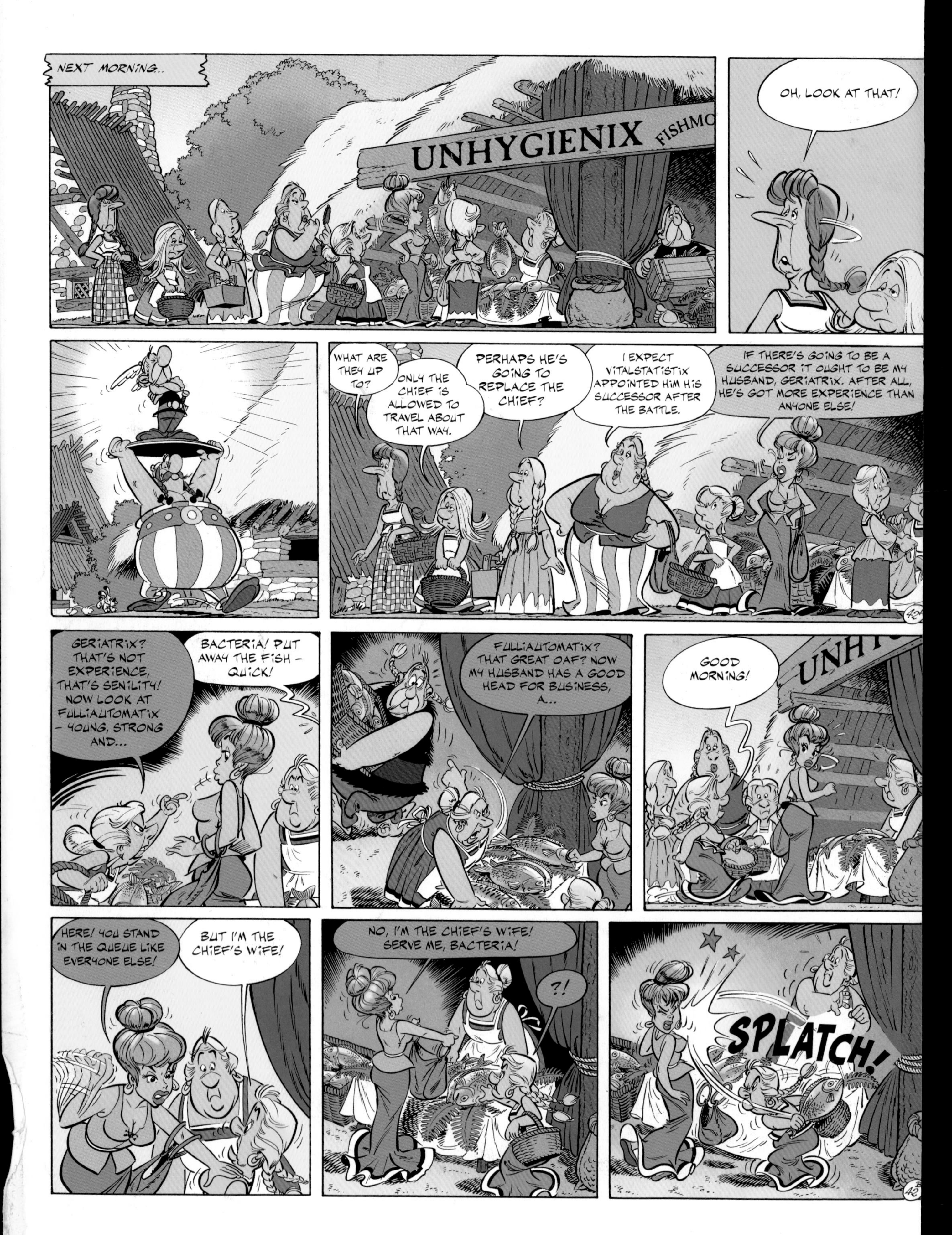
NEXT MORNING...
UNHYGIENIX
FISHMO
OH, LOOK AT THAT!
WHAT ARE THEY UP TO?
ONLY THE CHIEF IS ALLOWED TO TRAVEL ABOUT THAT WAY.
PERHAPS HE'S GOING TO REPLACE THE CHIEF?
I EXPECT VITALSTATISTIX APPOINTED HIM HIS SUCCESSOR AFTER THE BATTLE.
IF THERE'S GOING TO BE A SUCCESSOR IT OUGHT TO BE MY HUSBAND, GERIATRIX. AFTER ALL, HE'S GOT MORE EXPERIENCE THAN ANYONE ELSE!
GERIATRIX? THAT'S NOT EXPERIENCE, THAT'S SENILITY! NOW LOOK AT FULLIAUTOMATIX – YOUNG, STRONG AND...
BACTERIA! PUT AWAY THE FISH – QUICK!
FULLIAUTOMATIX? THAT GREAT OAF? NOW MY HUSBAND HAS A GOOD HEAD FOR BUSINESS, A...
GOOD MORNING!
HERE! YOU STAND IN THE QUEUE LIKE EVERYONE ELSE!
BUT I'M THE CHIEF'S WIFE!
NO, I'M THE CHIEF'S WIFE! SERVE ME, BACTERIA!
?!
SPLATCH!

CALM DOWN, CALM DOWN! WHAT'S GOING ON NOW?
BIFF!
BOFF!
CLONK!
UNI
I'LL TELL YOU WHAT'S GOING ON! THESE OLD BAGS ARE SAYING YOU'RE SENILE!
TEE HEE HEE!
OUCH!
BONG!
CHONK!
?
BUT I DIDN'T SAY A WORD!
I KNOW, BUT ALL THE SAME I CAN'T BRING MYSELF TO BASH THAT OLD RELIC!
43A
ME, AN OLD RELIC?
? ?
'VE GOT A RIGHT TO BE BASHED! I WANT TO BE BASHED!
I'LL BASH THE LOT OF YOU IF YOU DON'T LEAVE MY FISH ALONE!
ARE WE NEVER GOING TO HAVE ANY PEACE? STOP IT! THAT'S AN ORDER FROM YOUR CHIEF!
WHICH CHIEF?
THAT'S RIGHT. UNHYGIENIX IS CHIEF!
THAT IDIOT?
WELL, JULIUS CAESAR NEVER MADE THIS IDIOT A SENATOR!
BANG!
RRRUNCCH!
IFF!
NOW, NOW, WHAT'S ALL THIS ABOUT?
BONK!
BONK!
BON
43B

WHAT DO YOU THINK YOU'RE DOING ON THAT SHIELD?
THERE'S NO NEED TO RAISE THE ROOF...
...MINE'S A BIT LOW SO I THOUGHT I'D BETTER COME OUTSIDE TO ROADTEST THE SHIELD I'M GOING TO GIVE YOU.
ER... HA, HA! ... SEE YOU THIS EVENING, THEN...
THAT'S RIGHT...
UNHYGIENIX
FISHMONGER
I THINK THEY'VE GOT THE MESSAGE THIS TIME.
YES, THEY'RE FOND OF A FIGHT, IMPRACTICAL... ECCENTRIC... BUT YOU HAVE TO LIKE THEM. THEY'RE ONLY HUMAN!
THESE HUMANS ARE CRAZY!
TAP! TAP! TAP! TAP!
BUT THAT EVENING THE HUMANS HAVE FORGOTTEN THEIR TROUBLES, AND UNDER THE STARRY SKY WHICH COVERS THEM, WITH NO INTENTION OF FALLING ON THEIR HEADS, OUR FRIENDS THE GAULS ARE RE-UNITED FOR ONE OF THEIR TRADITIONAL BANQUETS, CELEBRATING, AMONG OTHER THINGS, THE END OF HOSTILITIES.
WHAT A WONDERFUL SURPRISE! MY DEAR FRIENDS, I AM AT A LOSS FOR WORDS...
UDERZO & GOSCINNY
THE END